Yan Tan Tether

Jane Burn

Indigo Dreams Publishing

First Edition: Yan Tan Tether
First published in Great Britain in 2020 by:
Indigo Dreams Publishing
24, Forest Houses
Cookworthy Moor
Halwill
Beaworthy
Devon
EX21 5UU

www.indigodreams.co.uk

Jane Burn has asserted her right under the Copyright, Designs and Patents Act 1988 to be identified as the author of this work.
© 2020 Jane Burn

ISBN 978-1-912876-25-9

British Library Cataloguing in Publication Data. A CIP record for this book can be obtained from the British Library.

This book is sold subject to the condition that it shall not, by way of trade or otherwise, be lent, re-sold, hired out, or otherwise circulated without the author's and publisher's prior consent in any form of binding or cover other than that in which it is published and without a similar condition including this condition being imposed on the subsequent purchaser.

Designed and typeset in Palatino Linotype by Indigo Dreams.
All images and artwork by the author © Jane Burn.
Printed and bound in Great Britain by 4edge Ltd.

Papers used by Indigo Dreams are recyclable products made from wood grown in sustainable forests following the guidance of the Forest Stewardship Council.

To Orca, Iggy, Patsy and all the other amazing creatures
who have shared their lives with me. Thank you
for all your years of friendship
and for allowing me to be included
in your brilliant world.

Acknowledgements

Life into the Light first published in Beltane, Three Drops from a Cauldron; *Were She Not Sunk* first published in Under the Radar: *Froghopper* first published in Butcher's Dog; *Badger on the Boyne* first published in The Curlew; *Trust a Spider's Web* first published on Zoomorphic; *Bogie Toad* commended in the 2019 Yorkmix Children's Poetry Competition; *Higgedy-Piggedy my Fair Hen* first published in The Emma Press Anthology of Love; *The birds told me stories of paths in the sky* first published on Clear Poetry; *Yan Tan Tether* first published on Diamond Twig; *Bad Luck Bird* first published on Clear Poetry; *Acorn* first published in The Fenland Reed; *Merry Christmas, Mixie Rabbit* first published on Ink, Sweat & Tears; *Nan wishes for snow* first published on The Poetry Shed.

Also by Jane Burn:

nothing more to it than bubbles
fAt aRouNd tHe MiddLe
Tongues of Fire

CONTENTS

Life into the Light 11

Therianthrope 12

Were She Not Sunk 15

Froghopper 16

Badger on the Boyne 18

Trust a Spider's Web 21

Bogie Toad 22

Higgedy-Piggedy, my Fair Hen 25

The birds told me stories of paths in the sky 26

Blinking up Dots of Early Sun 29

Yan Tan Tether 30

Sly Fox, Creep Fox, Hide Fox, Peep Fox 33

Bad-Luck Bird 34

Weirdly Localised Patch of Fog 37

Acorn 38

Mollusc Song 41

What we take for Love 42

Merry Christmas, Mixie Rabbit 45

Nan wishes for snow 46

There is no beginning without my end 49

Yan Tan Tether

Life into the Light

I heard the circle of spirits sing
for the change of season – *I am life*.
Saw them dance – the women
gentling out harmonics,
made as if to be nymphs,
huffing out the new day.
I saw them stamp to each beat
of Earth's eternal drum –
each trill of trunk-hid harpsichord,
each song of bud, splitting life into the light,
each long held note a new leaf
un-curdling its veined thin.
I see them marking time
through early dawn-spill,
see them wearing rings of broken sun,
see their feet, bare on wet grass.
The bulbs have slept – crocus
and snowdrop ask to slip their flesh.
Branches carry the quiver of nutlets,
asking to be born, blossom
an excitement as yet un-pinked.
I hear how they hope for renewal,
these gabble-witches, gorgeous
within their impish selves.
I hear how they hope for spring.

Therianthrope

The hours before dawn are a time
for peeling back my ill-fit people-skin,
for standing in its shed spill, for watching
my feet splatch into webs, pared flesh becoming
a sift of plume, a belly of down. The hours
before dawn are a time for looking down upon
worlds of cloud in water, of plunged moons –
for flying above this drowned heaven.
The hours before dawn are a time for the lightness

of my hollow bones, for a skirr of bliss, a glissade
of lake-land, the freshness of mistral bliss carried
upon me. Shapeshift, I keep the secret of a feather
in my palm. Every day, a quill loosed to the wind.
An offering – thankfulness for my time as a swan.
I watch it rise, a free thing. You do not know
that I have spikes of flight, ready under the shuck
of my frump. You do not hear my hush-hush heart,
silent through the day – waiting for the night.

Were She Not Sunk

They say there is magic. They are right.
I am Queen of the forest – my feet are green,
stomach a barrel of love and grief. I stand
at a pool and see that it carries my look-like.
She gestures at me, ruler as she is of the other-world –
my opposite, my twin we kneel at water's edge,

touch palm to palm, a slither of mirrored cool
slipped between us. I frown, she frowns.
We tinkle laughter, sometimes cry – willow leaves
upon the liquid skin as we top up the level with tears.
I would wipe them for her, were she not sunk
and I flesh. Her body is slit by a moorhen's

knife-edged stream – my sister takes time to re-form
breast and neck, so capable was the cutting.
I show her birds – nests scribbled on boughs
like scratched out eyes. Some filled with shells –
I count the empty ones and cry for loss. Oak and owl,
their time passed in shedding nuts and spitting bone –

badger on grub, feast in fallen wood. Thicker inside,
where trunks will bare allow the passing of slender deer
and light is measured out in thinner beams. A whisper
goes nowhere. Hollow, some of them – opened
into coffins, hearts gone. Here, in such tangled core
are kept the secrets. Here are the deeper things.

Froghopper

Mammy born us in spit wash – bubbled eggs!
She stuck us to lavender so we could lick
the stink off perfumed sap,
be bred in the purple, like majesties.
Inside we was small and lettuce-frail,
tiny ink-pen dotty motes
for eyes, peepy-black,
spun sugar hairs on us heads.
Frogs paddling a slavered den.
A hockle-home – a man's disgust to touch us
is the way we grows up safe.
Fit as fleas, green as peas.
Cuckoo clears its pipes –
gizzards us a lully-bye
we never tires of hearing.
Two notes – *hoo! hoo!* to whistle us
a witchy scud. Time for foamy beds
you bugs. Time for shaping skin
and sprouting wings.

Badger on the Boyne

I sail to catch the Prince of the river,
nestled in willow, bobbed in hide, trawling
for salmon to eat myself wise. *Come to my hook,
thou pretty silver fish!* His shape, tempting-slick
under boat skin – I have spent my life wishing
on mouthfuls of hazelnut. Just one lick
of your shining sides is all I need, I swear.
Then I shall be King of all Creatures!
Great FinTan, if I cannot eat you then perhaps
you can spare a kiss? I will keep my teeth
behind my lips, promise I will not bite.
Not a nip of your sweet sushi sides! If only
I could know what you know! I would use it
for good, would rule with velvet paws.
I would be kind. My coracle would be solid gold,
reflecting sun in its cup as I bask, furry and royal
in sable skin, a diamond crown put rakish
on my skull, for how should I be king
without one, eh? Voles on the banks
shall worship as I pass – I shall keep a harem
of birds above my head. They shall sing
my passing in proclamations of squawk.
*Bow down! Here sails the majesty of all
our Earth – benevolence in ev'ry hair! Behold!
For he carries the mark of angels striped
upon his head!* That slick – he turns
his eyeballs from the deep and laughs
at my grandiose ideal, bubbles like balls of glass.
I will get your wisdom yet! I shake my fist.
It is just a matter of widening my net.

Trust a Spider's Web

Weaver. Warp and wefter, twilling busy – when the wind
unpegs my work I spin again, wet my lips. Count
the silk-stuck bundles,

taste their necks with hypodermic teeth, kiss my venom in.
Suckable! So eatable! My tongue-buds wet as I
anticipate their vitals –

drinking up a gnat, straining juices from a yum-bug,
I get me round and fat. Dream of babies,
spiderlings crawling the zags,

following them like pathways to my heart. I can wait.
Fill the time with tatting, fingers threading picots.
He will come – will answer to my pluck

of pizzicato music. We will complect, wind the dawn,
wake dew, dandle its cabochon light. And then I'll eat him –
I have had my use. He is only seeds.

My children float on loosened strands, froth to catch on
rearing stamen, fence-post tops. Snag their fibril parachutes
until they find their place, begin a den.

Spin – spit out your satin, snag what blows in with tomorrow.
Plait you web with prayer and hope for spoil. There is
treasure in the air. Just catch.

Bogie Toad

has a face like a welly boot toe,
eyes like soapy moons, blinky caps of lid,
no use for lashes. Mouth all smiley split –
curled inside a roly-poly, roly-poly,
roly-poly tongue, long as a mile,
fast as twenty lightnings, sticky-stuck,
lick its own forehead, in and out!
Catching all them yumptious bugs,
legs and wings and everything –
taste of liquorice, dead-fly pie
all wriggle-taste. Delicious wasps!
Skin like teabags, leafy, leatherbound
stretchy-wetchy, twixy-tween his toes,
knobble-burp, rock-back,
windbag, gribbit bubble
throat sing, leg, leg, bounce, bounce,
hopper-flash, jump. Floated jelly eggs
in a mish-mash, tadpole blisters,
babies waggling from their snotty pods
to river freedom, every one of them
croaking joy. *Uuuuuuuurgle-buuuurgle.*
Graaaaak! Brrrrrrrrrrt-brrrrrrrrrrrrrt,
flip-flop, leap-frog, rubber-foot boing!

Higgedy-Piggedy, my Fair Hen

I sing to my sweet-bird, sweet-heart, sweet-nest,
sweet-breast, sweet-stomach down on our ovalled
young. Sometimes nine, sometimes ten, our happy
omens in albumen. Little tick-tick of forming yolks,
snug in a calcium spot-skin of fragile wall. Tail-grow,
leg-grow, lung-grow, head-grow – all the while,
my gull-wife's lullaby croon. Grow calm, grow
good, grow lovely in your orby traps. Turn them,
turn them tadpoles, eating up the yellow gold.

Eat yourself, my petrel-Queen, I tell to the urchin
of mine eyes. I will sit thee time enough to swag
your creamy crop with gullet-fish, gizzard-silver,
slip down, lovely codlings. Take the sky, re-open
yourself to the salt air, bring back a nursery rhyme
for our chicklings new-formed ears. Chant them,
spell them into being – soak the knowing of oceans
through them shells. Come back to me – our love
is an albatross. It will not bear halving.

Our clutch, with its bare grip on cliff is woken,
faddling with egg-tooth on husk – the time will soon
be now. What falls from this sheer will be mourned.
What lives will be fed on belly's silt. She is back,
my fallen star – we beak our needs, clatter to swear
fidelity again. She preens and dips her bullet head.
I swap my place with her and she feathers down.
My voice is the scrape of rock on rock to the world
but to her, the ecstasy of togetherness, joy of us.

The birds told me stories of paths in the sky

Wrens make stump-tailed secrets. Hedgerow dabs
in their doily baskets – Home Sweet Homes to peep from,
dainty, plump as busy fairies. They will show the art
of quick-flits, how to zip quick-sharp from leaf to leaf.
Come sing with the passerines! The dawn opens
to their throats. Beady fatlings, little smut of herringbone
on their wings. Go higher! Crows have a little more ambition –
you will find them, murder grouped in the twig-tops.
Corvids, fed on feasts of flesh and berries – any chance
to get their beaks down, stuff their guts. Stick with them,
survive! They do not wait for cats to make lunch
of their meats. Their bills are smirking slate –
they are suckers for shiny and sweet. Go higher still!
Swans, so pure in the air – how beautiful, how beautiful!
They are poetry. Even their deaths are blood and snow.
They will tell you of matings and babies, of staying together
for life. Such fairness! All water reflects them, *Children of Lir* –
their spectacle in the air, their flight is song. So elegant,
as they skim on glass, making sweet hearts of their necks.
Be brave enough to join the *Gyps Rueppellii*. In days way back,
man cricked his neck, called them angels. They fly where air
meets ozone – come to troposphere! Beauty matters not
when they can bite through bone. Heads bald as blind-worms,
scapula lugged like menhir on their backs. No other bird
gets up so close to heaven. They go from carcass to sky,
rot to redemption, hunch to halleluiah!

Blinking up Dots of Early Sun

The horse's eyes said everything and nothing – them and me, we are masters of middle distance.

All we could ever need to know is hidden here, at the point where squint meets horizon.

We take our breaths together, bellies big with long, slow ones in. Pause to peer again,

cover our vision with lids, breathe out. One of them touches my arm with his nose, *bump bump*.

This is how they ask me questions. *Yes*, I say. But I don't know what I mean. Another drops

his coffin head to grass but does not eat – we are too wary of monsters over the hill.

Wherever I move, they follow, these skins of muscle. Shine makes rings on a skewbald back.

Bump bump. They are still waiting for my answer.

Yan Tan Tether

Beauty Swaledales, faces sooty like they's dipped in t' cole 'ole;
eyes rimmed white as if we see'd a ghost.
Necks all wriggled wi' kemp, coats all clotted cream;
we does not live in want. Grass, deep to us piebald knees – us
farmer brings us in to lamb. Coddles t' poddy, chases out ked.
Come t' year's end, tups raddle us backs, kindle us wombs –
we feels them, little growing things and wonder this time if
we gets to keep 'em more than five month.
See 'em grow to hoggets, shearlings, bonny gimmers –
get some babbies of their own so I be grandma.
Nowt but chewy mutton, old yow counting all her grandlings –
yan, tan, tether, mether, pip. I be yanadick – I wonders how
long I has left 'ere on this fell. I be broken-mouthed

yet manage – maybe mester will draft me to sweeter parts
and finer blades. Plenty time left. I am a wick 'un yet.
Hefted on these pastures, we seek not to wander far –
chew cuddy and stand in t' wind. We isn't nesh,
we does not mind it siling down. Walls spit their stone
along the moor in moss-topped tumble. We lie on t' lee side
for storms. Reflect us-selves, dabble lips in overflowing pools,
sup on syrup. We only needs to look to Heaven and it cries
us rain. I listens to t' hymn of curlews, hiding pebbledash –
the skrike of grouse hid in meadowsweet. Bees, grazing
the bogbean think of honey – sun laps across t' moor
in chunks of gold and every hiker passing takes a breath
and tells how *this* be God's own country.

Sly Fox, Creep Fox, Hide Fox, Peep Fox

Sly fox, creep fox, hide fox, peep fox –
wind your sinews through the dark,
tawnyhead. Pant through your running
with quiet breath, empty the heat

from your lungs, make clouds all misty
in the night. Paws small as coins, dainty
spot of spoor sometimes left in soft ground,
mostly left none at all, your step so light.

The moon on your bristled back, nose
to rabbits trail – eat to live, not live to eat.
Got to brew your milk – three little cubs,
waiting back at the den like rolled fuzz,

whining for teats. You lost your love to the roadside –
screamed when you saw the waste of his
writhed corpse. Your heart was breached.
Bone fox, break fox, grieve fox, ache fox.

Tread careful, vixen-red. Those that hunt you
raise up a hunger of dogs to run you to ground,
ride their beasts to wrongness – un-rode horses never
hungered for your meat. Curbed with steel and spurred

with heel they cut the fields with iron-skim feet.
You shake your coney-meal, cache for later under leaves,
find your babies, settle snug and pray for peace.
Safe fox, sleep fox, dream fox, deep fox.

Bad-Luck Bird

One for sorrow.
One little piebald augur of doom loafing the road,
a shiftless portent. It knows what it's doing – bracing
its ribby toes like jacks, stilting on tinder-stick legs.
One in your rear view mirror, *one*
scratting along your morning pavement. *One*
dropping gutter-moss on your clear, plastic porch roof.
Two for joy –
winking their marmalade eyes, wiping sticky fur
from greedy beaks, licking round their smiles.
Joy indeed, on this carrion feast.
We are happy, gorged on maggot meat, mated for life.
Why this happiness in pairs?
I have had my woe from being doubled up
and I have sat alone, feeling that bit closer to the stars.
Three for a girl –
you already wasted your shibboleth on me.
Four for a boy!
Don't you dare turn your sight to my son –
I tell him nothing of you. Your anathema will end here.
Five for silver, six for gold –
robbed from the very eyes of the dead
should you wish to collect it, I bet.
Seven four our secrets?
I already know that you are night and day, thief.
I know the meaning of your solitary forms,
know that if I see you on your own,
then you have lost your loves.

Weirdly Localised Patch of Fog

Autumn's days have fallen under a chilled spell.
    Underneath my layers I shiver, briskly rub

my hands. A grim, weirdly localised patch
    of fog has settled in a dusky valley,

dipped between the grassy meet of two
    sloped fields. I watch its nucleus leech out,

grey tendrils shifting cunningly over
    the plough – spooky, oppressive, cold.

It smokes, wafts, seeps. Like a phantom's
    gathering, death nymphs loosed, or a

dusty, moth-eaten bridal veil cast over
    jilted ground. Ashes vacating the lungs

of an Earth giant, exhumed. A sudden fluster
    bloats my coat, lifts my scarf, mixes my hair

with leaves. Strong enough to lift me, almost – carry me
    into the fog. Drizzle clings to wool in fuzzy drops.

Acorn

Ripened, we fall – *dop, dop!*
Litter the floor with our souls, tiny tumble-nuts
casting ourselves down – unfastened from the tree,
exuviated children, little-hatted, merry-pipkin,
fairy-titfer hazel shiners. Pods in a cupule pixie dish –
children's finger toppers, thumbs in bonnets.
Snouty pig, furrowing with hopeful nose, *yum-yum, snuff!*
Smelling out our squirrel-fingered shiny pericape shells,
nestled as we are in winter-ready cache.
Our little plumules tucked away, all sleepy
'till we find some muck to work our magic –
waiting, patient for the rain's quench,
the nod of the sun. We can be butterflies,
unfurling our cotyledon to the light.
We ask the jay to carry us, scatter-pip
so we can make new forest, send our sapling shoots
of fresh wood poking, wriggling bodkin-foot
into the forest floor. Raise a canopy between
ground and sky – swell our circumference
of heartwood, quest our root and offer
green-blood leaf, to shelter and shade.
How willingly we offer our throats to the doe –
pain for a moment, then the pleasure of feeding,
feeling her velvet lips.

We can make new forest, our sapling

Still I find a was to dance

Mollusc Song

Naked conch, a homeless periwinkle. I am bald, cowering
under carapace, exposed to every careless tread –
I cannot withdraw the softer parts. You snails have shells
to slip to, wind your heads through whorls, coiled safe
from bird beak, snug away from claw. I would run if could
in my blistered skin – bubbled leather land-lock limpet!
Legless, yet still I find a way to dance!

I will balter for my mate in the moist leaf-mulch –
I wish he would join me in my phylum on the floor.
My prayer is phlegm. Measuring mudflat moon-steps
I have minutes for years, my seconds are hours. I can live
lifetimes in a day. The music is the gentle in-and-outing
of my pneumostome. Just one lung but I can air-full suck it,
gape the blow-hole on my neck, breathe it in and oboe-out.

A melancholy tune of low notes, rallentando slow notes,
hear them in the dirt below notes. I polish my oily mantle,
hope he reads me in my ooze. I keep myself wet
for fear of desiccation – I do not want to die by crumbling.
I disgust myself, but how I want my clutch
of slime-slipped eggs! If I cannot have them, salt.
I'll cry my own end with tears.

What we take for Love

I wonder what I believe in, somedays.
Umbrellas, yes. If you learn to never
leave the house without one, you will never
get wet. Don't open them indoors, mind. You

can live without bad luck. Little wisdoms –
seven years for a broken mirror. Give
a penny for someone's thoughts – if you think
you can live with what you learn from them. Milk

is something to cry for, spilled. It's like snow
when winter is come, like a lake of silk, folding into the
table's grain. I believe in birds – their flight,
their murmurations written on the sky

at dusk a sight for sore eyes. On the ground,
one feather – plain, from a sparrow. Beauty
is measured by a beholder's sight – I
pluck its tiny wisp from the grass. Inside

it lie the secrets of heaven. They might
rub off on me if I clutch tight enough.
Lamps take away night but the heart stays dark.
This is what we have mistaken for love.

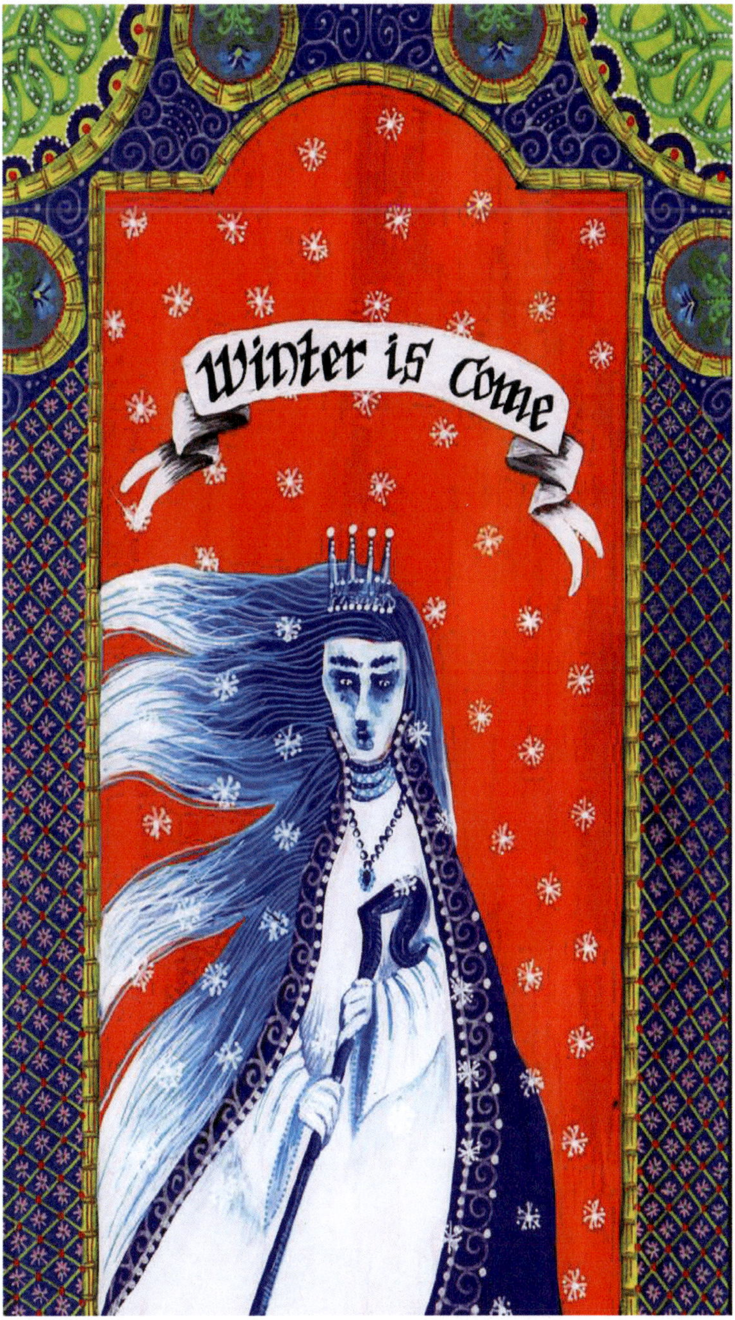
Winter is Come

joy at the coming

Merry Christmas, Mixie Rabbit

Mistletoe furls from hawthorn, apple and oak, births
its berries – each one a bubble of snow, a blister of milk.
Birds lift them off with a beaky kiss, relish their burst
of bliss. The bared timbers sleep, hearts tucked and dreamy
inside, deep. For them a biding – the patient knowledge
of next year's buds, of baby leaves. For the evergreens,
a show of plush against the spangle of frost, joy
at the coming ascension of night and the soon-wearing
of stars along their arms – a clarity of tar-blue air balanced
between needled hands. In the sharp of dusk,
the drunk smell of winter haylage, pungent dung.
Bundled in a nook of roots is a hazel body, mute as a stone.
Blind and clinging to this illusion of safety, the dogs
see it long before me. Fix their murder upon it,
ask to be unleashed. As we pass, it feels the shake
of the path beneath our feet, hears our noisy breath –
the best it can do is hold still, try to un-scrunch
its pink-stuck eyes. It is praying for invisibility, for us to pass.
When twilight comes, a fox will take the rabbit,
quick and quiet as flight. The trees, bald or fleshed
with green will swallow its small cry. The berries
will shine cold as moons. I hope for succour
for those that hurt – peace for hearts that beat through the dark.
Let drifts be kind to whatever lies frozen below.
Let the coming year open its face to light.
May pity be shown to all defenceless things.

Nan wishes for snow

so she can welcome a world of spilled milk.
She will blemish it with petals, stretch the scrag
of her neck. Feel it flaked with crystals,
each drift of them a test of the Almighty's skill.
Hear the first of its fall, far away; collect
the sound in skin-soft scoops. *There*, she will sigh,
detecting the little pliffs. *Here it comes*.
Her udder tucked, pink with cold –

worth the exposure to be outside,
on untouched acres, begging for first foot.
The sound will be the gentle ring of winter –
the land will wake, robin will clutch the fencepost,
blink his blackberry eye. She will reach her tongue,
imagine tasting his cardinal stain, her smile
a split of snaggle-tooth, laugh of underbite.
Strange yet radiant in the dawn.

strange yet radiant

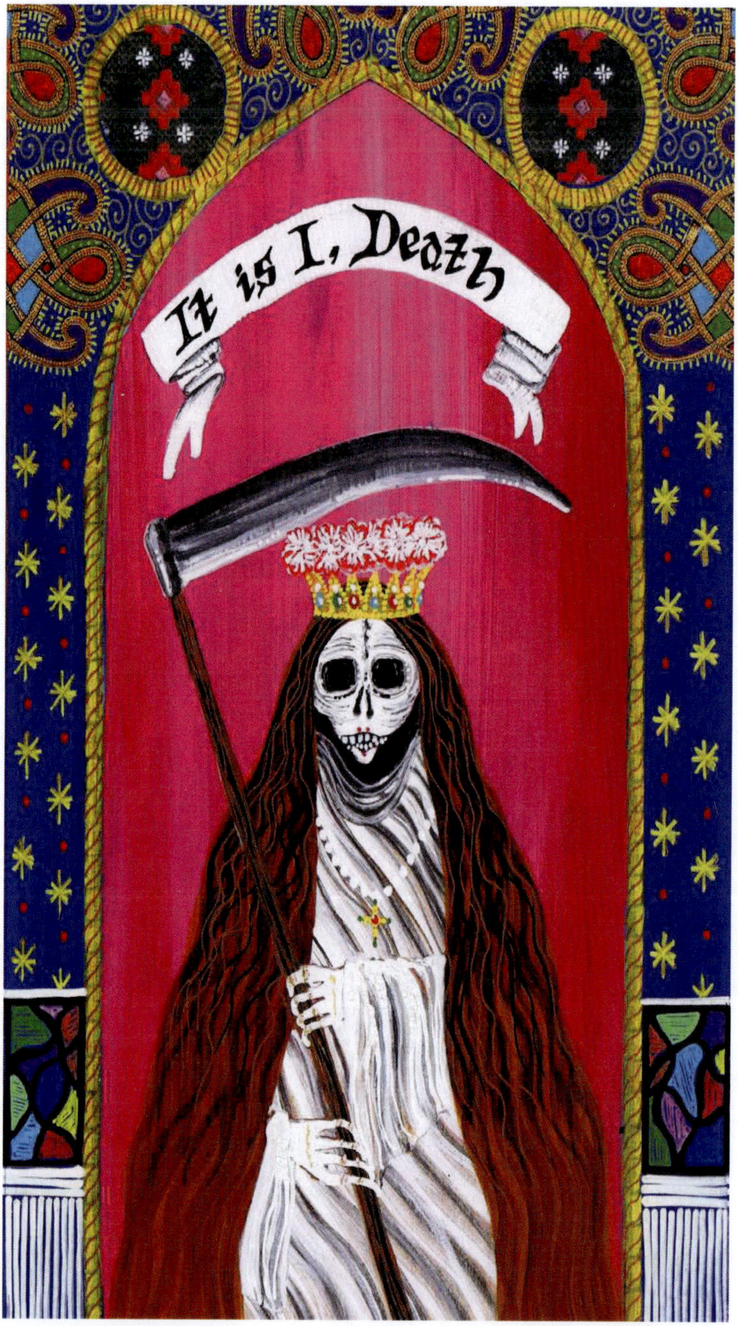
It is I, Death

There is no beginning without my end

no start, no finish, no bits in between
    without my patient waiting. No new growth
unless there is withering first, no new leaves
    unless the last ones fall, no thaw unless
the snow melts away. This is nature's order – fox
    cannot feed without rabbit, cat without mouse,
hawk without pigeon, bird without worm.
    Seconds, minutes, hours, days and weeks all pass,
never to be recaptured – time works to my whim.
    You cannot stop its passing. I am rarely welcome –
too early it seems, always. Wrong time, wrong person,
    wrong manner, wrong place. Sometimes,
there is just no reasoning me out. Some are ready
    to come to my arms – I hold them and promise
my watchfulness over their bones. *It is I, Death* –
    I come to them gentle, if ever I can – lift the body
of a shattered hare from the roadside, weep
    over hedgehog, mourn for flowers, cut and wilting
in a vase. I cannot claim your memories – they will live
    as constellations above your head. I cannot claim
your love. But you see, I am inevitable – as day
    is quashed by night, as bank is eroded by river, slow.

Indigo Dreams Publishing Ltd
24, Forest Houses
Cookworthy Moor
Halwill
Beaworthy
Devon
EX21 5UU
www.indigodreams.co.uk